Muddypaws

Goes to School

D0490650

Written by Peter Bently
Illustrated by Simon Mendez

First published by Parragon in 2011

Parragon
Chartist House
15 – 17 Trim Street
Bath BA1 1HA, UK
www.parragon.com

Copyright © Parragon Books Ltd 2011

All rights reserved. No part of this publication may be reproduced,
stored in a retrieval system or transmitted, in any form or by any means,
electronic, mechanical, photocopying, recording or otherwise, without
the prior permission of the copyright holder.

ISBN 978-1-4454-3017-1

Printed in China

Muddypaws

Goes to School

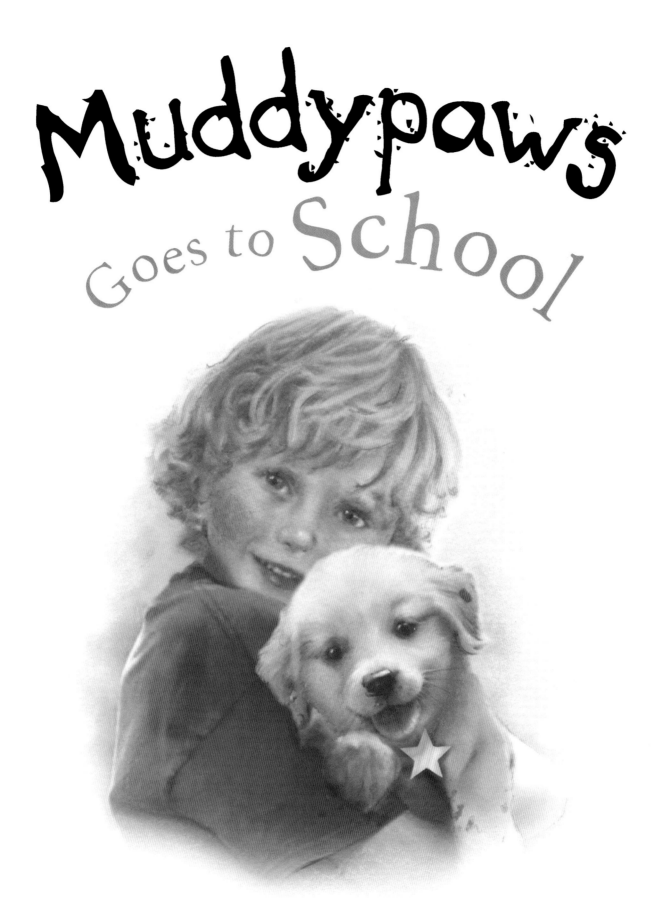

Bath · New York · Singapore · Hong Kong · Cologne · Delhi
Melbourne · Amsterdam · Johannesburg · Auckland · Shenzhen

Ben and his puppy, Muddypaws, did everything together.
They played inside...

they explored outside...

and at the end of the day they cuddled up together.

Wherever Ben went, Muddypaws went too.

"Except for school," smiled Ben, as Muddypaws popped a bubble.

"And my bath!"

Next day, Ben was late for school.
"See you later, Muddypaws!" he cried.
Uh-oh! Ben forgot to shut the gate!

Wherever Ben goes, I go too!

When Muddypaws padded into school he couldn't see Ben anywhere.

He mooched merrily in the nature corner...

and then **lolloped** off to the painting corner.

SQUIDGE!
went the red.

SQUIRT!
went the
yellow and green.

SQUIRT!
went the blue.

What fun! thought Muddypaws.

"What a mess!" gasped the teacher.
But where was Muddypaws?

Muddypaws was looking for Ben in the school garden.
He didn't find Ben but he did find a spade.
But I can dig with my paws! he thought.

SCRITCH-SCRATCH!

SCRITCH-SCRATCH!

SCRITCH-SCRATCH!

Muddypaws dug and dug and dug.

Digging is hard work! yawned Muddypaws. Here's a nice cosy spot for a nap.

"Oh no!" gasped the teacher at break. "Who has made all this mess? They've buried all the flowers in sand!"

Muddypaws woke up with a bump.

wheeeeeee!!

he thought.

I'm going for a ride! Perhaps I'll find Ben on the way.

Ben was upside-down on the climbing frame.
"Hey!" he said. "That trailer's got a tail!"

But when he looked again the trailer was empty.

Muddypaws had sniffed something tasty.

Yummy! A snack!

Back in class, Amy started to sob.
"She's lost her toy puppy!" said Ben.
"Don't worry, Amy," said the teacher. "We'll all help to find it."

The children hunted inside…

...and outside.

"Here it is, Amy!" cried Ben. But what was Amy giggling at?

"You found my puppy!" smiled Amy.

"And you found mine!" laughed Ben. "Hello
Muddypaws! What are you doing at school?"

Muddypaws trotted home with Ben, proudly
wearing the star that teacher had made him.

"Teacher says your name should be Mischief, not Muddypaws!" said Ben.

"But I love you just the same!"

THE END